EVE BUNTING

I Am the Mummy HEB-NEFERT

Illustrated by
DAVID CHRISTIANA

VOYAGER BOOKS
HARCOURT, INC.

San Diego   New York   London

A **nomarch** (´nä-märk) is the chief magistrate of a province of ancient Egypt.

Text copyright © 1997 by Eve Bunting
Illustrations copyright © 1997 by David Christiana

www.harcourt.com

First Voyager Books edition 2000
Voyager Books is a registered trademark of Harcourt, Inc.

The Library of Congress has cataloged the hardcover edition as follows:
Bunting, Eve, 1928–
I am the mummy Heb-Nefert/written by Eve Bunting; illustrated by David Christiana.
p. cm.
Summary: A mummy recalls her past life in ancient Egypt as the beautiful wife of the pharoah's brother.
[1. Mummies—Fiction. 2. Egypt—Civilization—To 332 B.C.—Fiction.] I. Christiana, David, ill. II. Title.
PZ7.B91527Iam 1997
[Fic]—dc20   95-46927
ISBN 0-15-200479-3

ISBN 0-15-202464-6 pb

C E G H F D

The illustrations in this book were done in watercolors on Arches hot press watercolor paper.
The display type was hand-lettered by Lloyd Kirkpatrick.
The text type was set in Spectrum.
Color separations by Bright Arts, Ltd., Singapore
Printed and bound by Tien Wah Press, Singapore
Production supervision by Ginger Boyer
Designed by Lisa Peters

To my family. You are all so beautiful.

— E. B.

For Kristie

— D. C.

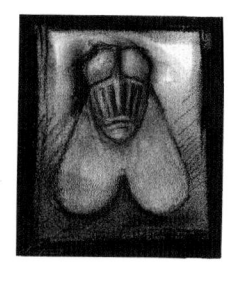

I AM THE mummy Heb-Nefert,

black as night,

stretched as tight

as leather on a drum.

My arms are folded

on my hollow chest

where once my live heart beat.

My ears are holes

that hear no sound.

Once I was the daughter of a nomarch,

favored, beautiful.

But all things change.

I danced one evening for the pharaoh's brother, Ti.
My pleated linen robe
swayed gentle at my every step.
The circlet on my head
gleamed with its jeweled light.
My eyes, my hands
gave promises of bliss
that made him weak.
And soon he loved me.

I was a cherished wife.
The palace was my home.
I lived for him and he for me.

Handmaidens dressed me every day.
They kept my head so sweetly shaved,
pumiced and polished till it shone.
They painted me with yellow dye,
darkened the lashes of my eyes with kohl,
shadowed my lids with blue,
the color of the evening sky.
My nails were hennaed red as jasper beads,
my flaxen wig was jewel woven.
And on the top
a cone of scented fat
melted to liquid in the summer warmth
and smelled of flowers.
I was so beautiful.
But these things pass.

We sailed upon the Nile,
my lord and I,
the wildfowl rising from the reeds
along the bank,
the ripples of the sacred river
soft against our boat.
Sometimes we saw a hippopotamus,
great jaws agape,
a crocodile.
But we were ever safe.

At times my husband threw a stick
to bring the winged birds down.
My cat, well trained in gentleness,
would run along the banks
and fetch them back.
So good a cat, Nebut!
My husband, swift and strong,
he seldom missed.

We'd wander in the gardens, he and I,
beside the pleasure lake
where lotus blossoms grew.
The servant girls would come
on soundless feet
and bring us fruit — grapes, dates, and figs —
the baskets balanced on their heads,
a cloth of linen spread
beneath a canopy that kept us from the sun.
And we would feast
while harpists played.

One day, disguised,
my handmaiden and I
went back to where I once had lived
before the pharaoh's brother loved me.

I watched the women crushing wheat
to make the bread.
I saw the men hoeing the fields,
the boys beside them
using stones in slings
to scare the birds away.

I saw the house where I was born.
My parents gone now
but the snake still there,
still tightly coiled and sleek
inside its kitchen basket.
Sleepy
but, I knew, alert,
to keep the rats and mice away
from where the grain was stored.
The same snake or another.
Who could tell?

I wept a little,
but I knew my life was good,
so good, beside my lord.

My golden cat, Nebut, I loved.
She loved me, too,
and came with me
into the silent twilight of the afterlife
when day changed to eternity.

I rose above myself
and watched.

I watched as they
anointed me with oils and spices,
took away the parts of me
that were inside,
and filled me up
with natron, cinnamon, and herbs.
My eyes were closed and plugged.
Beeswax filled my nose.
They capped my nails with gold
studded with precious stones,
bejeweled me from head to toe,
and bound me up in linen,
layer on layer.
I was to be
for all eternity
well kept for him.

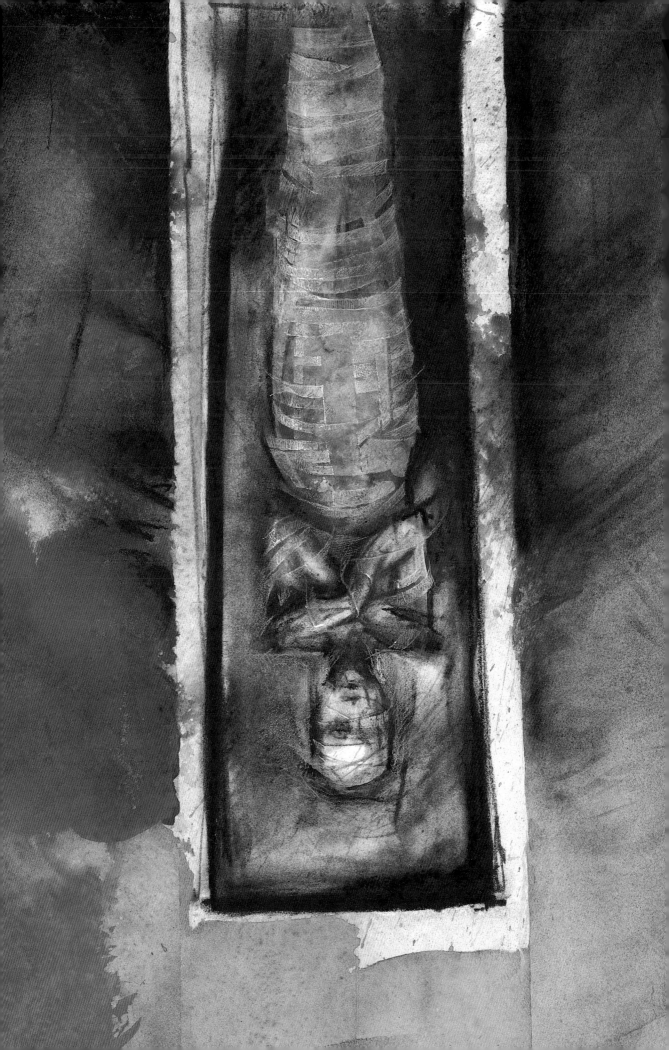

They made a mask
painted to look like me,
bound up my cat and masked her, too,
my faithful cat, Nebut.
Placed me in my sarcophagus
pictured around with likenesses
of gods who would receive me.

The sled that took me to my tomb
was pulled by oxen.

Behind, the lines of weepers wept
and sprinkled dust about their heads
to show their grief.
Porters carried things that I would need,
the food that I would eat,
my jewels, amulets, my offerings to the gods.

Great golden Horus, Falcon in the Sky,
awaited me,
and he would greet
the barge that bore me
through the streams of stars.

I would be blessed.

They placed me gently in the tomb,
juniper berries at my head and feet,
my gilded cat, Nebut, to stay with me.

My dear lord wept.
The pharaoh said
an amulet
would bear his brother's name and mine.
The world would know
we two had loved.

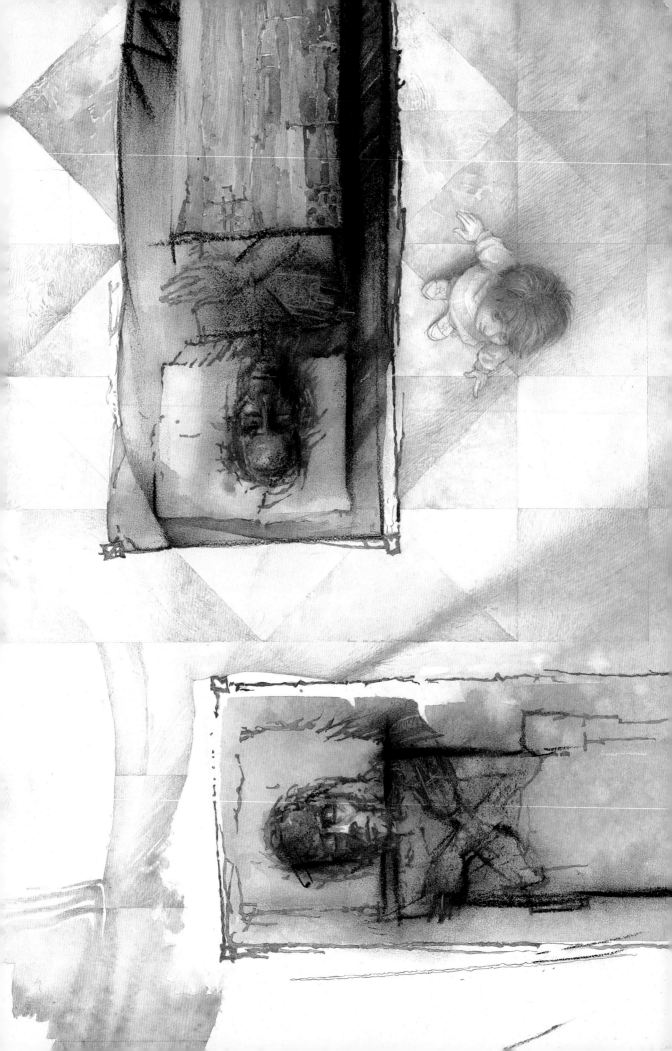

My Noble One grew old

and also left that life

to lie at last beside me

in the night that followed night.

Time passed and time,

dark time and years,

till we were found,

our bodies moved,

placed in glass coffins

under lights

in quiet rooms.

I rose above myself and watched

as people came.

They peered into the cases where we lay.

They spoke,
the words unknown to me
but understood as they were said.
"This was a person? This . . . and this?"

How foolish that they do not see
how all things change,
and so will they.
Three thousand years from now
they will be dust and bones.
I am the mummy Heb-Nefert,
black as night,
stretched as tight
as leather on a drum.

Once I was beautiful.